BY FRANK VIVA

HarperCollins*PublishersLtd*

To these ten remarkable women: Julia (my best friend), Camille and Mia (I meant to read this to you when you were much younger), Charlotte, Susan, and Barbara (thank you for this book), Delphine, Laura, Tilly, and Sophia (a new generation of book lovers)

Published by HarperCollins Publishers Ltd
First Canadian Edition

HarperCollins Publishers Ltd. 2 Bloor Street East, 20th Floor, Toronto, Ontario, Canada M4W 1A8

HarperCollins books may be purchased for educational, business, or sales promotional use through our Special Markets Department.

ISBN 978-1-44340-620-8

9 8 7 6 5 4 3 2 1 • IM Printed in China

www.harpercollins.ca

Library and Archives Canada Cataloguing in Publication information is available

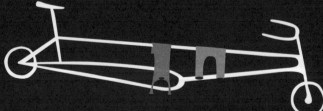

This book was created as a single, continuous thirty-five-foot-long piece of art using Adobe Illustrator. It was printed on 140gsm Gold Sun Woodfree. The words were set in Neutraface Text, and the display type was hand drawn by Frank Viva.

ALONG A LONG
ROAD

Along a long

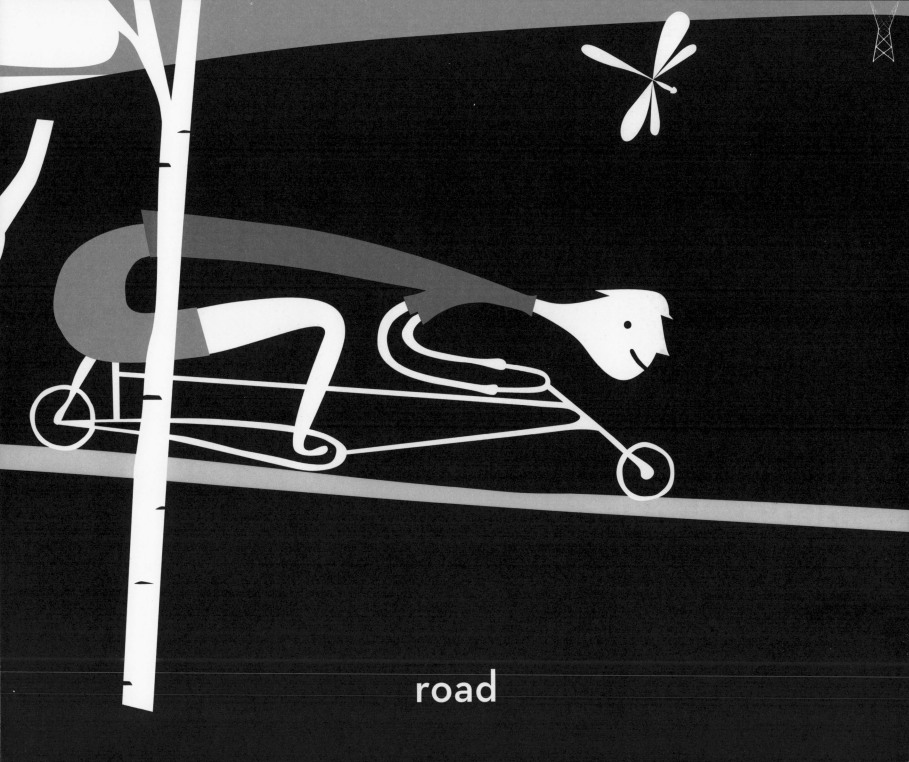

road

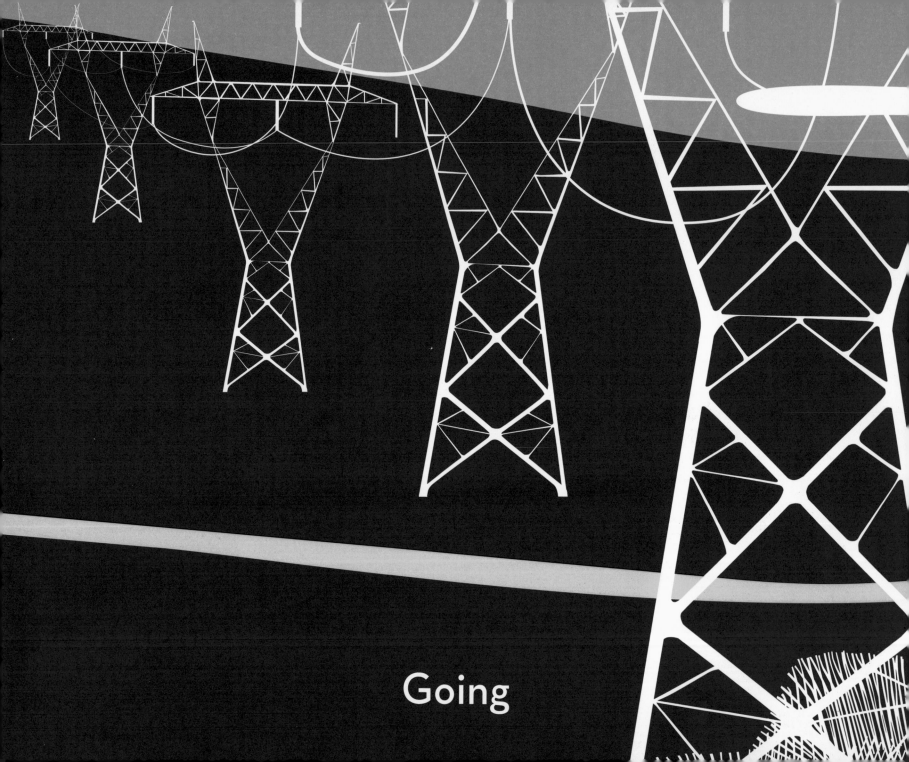

Going

up

Around a small town

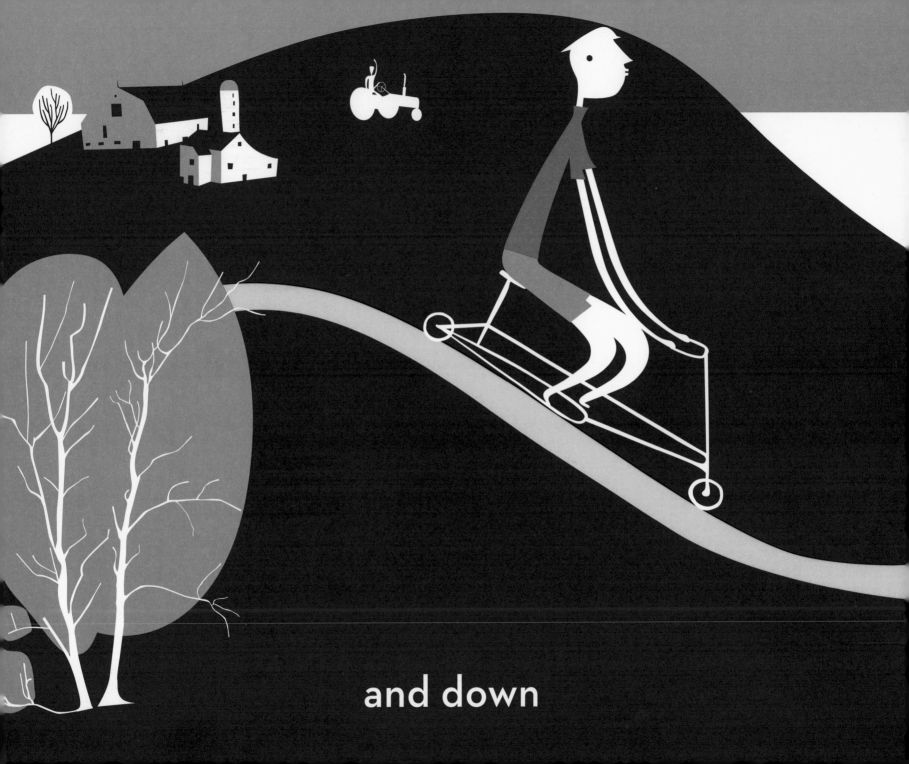

and down

Into

a tunnel

And

out

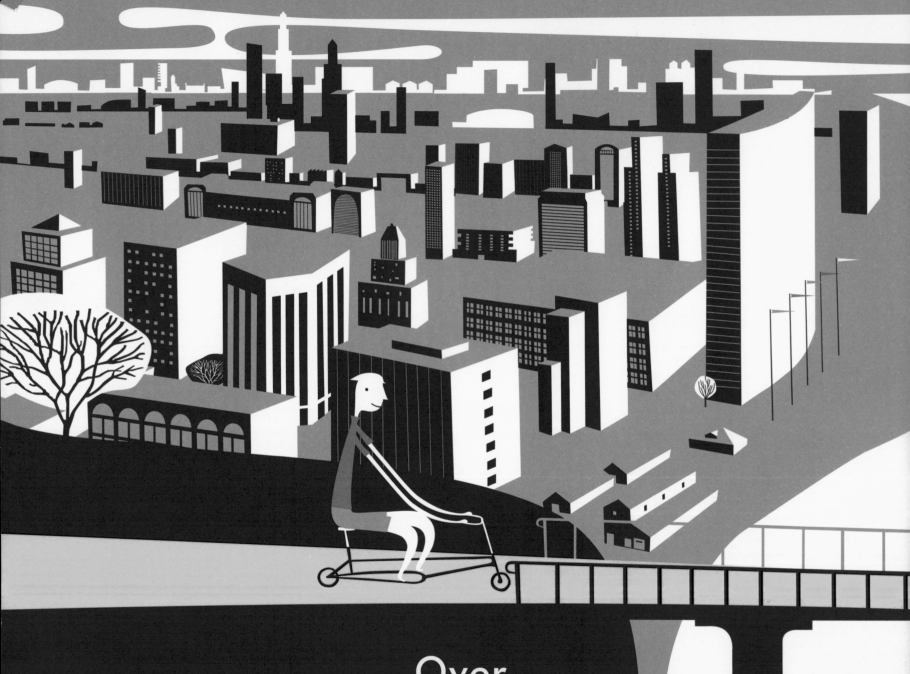

Over

a bridge

One, two,

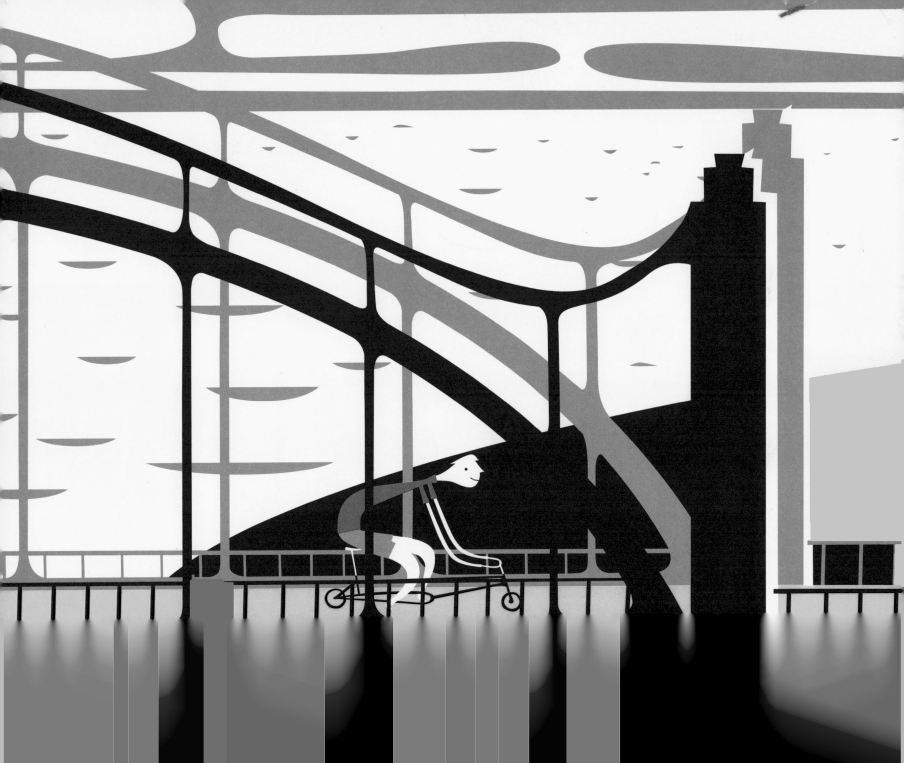

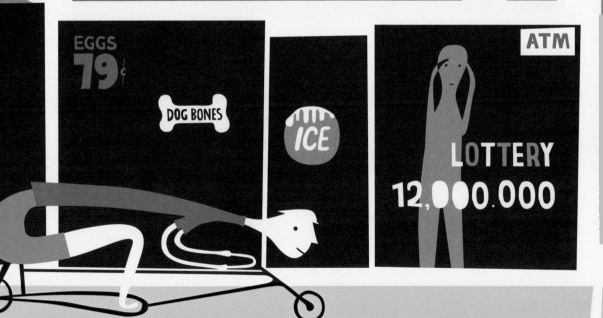

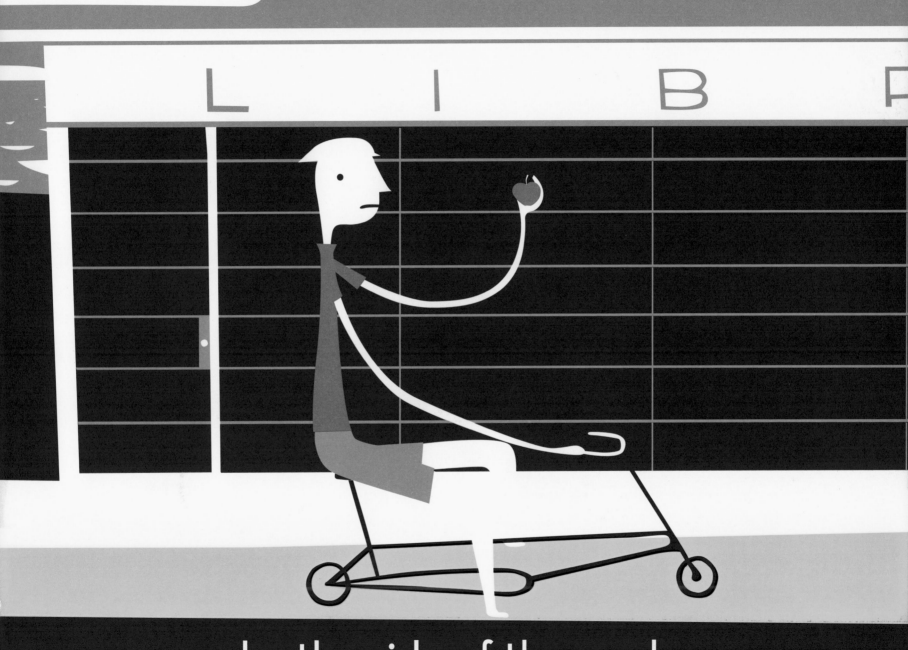

by the side of the road

Up again

back on the track

Along a long road

going fast

Around a round bend

near the end

And start all over

again

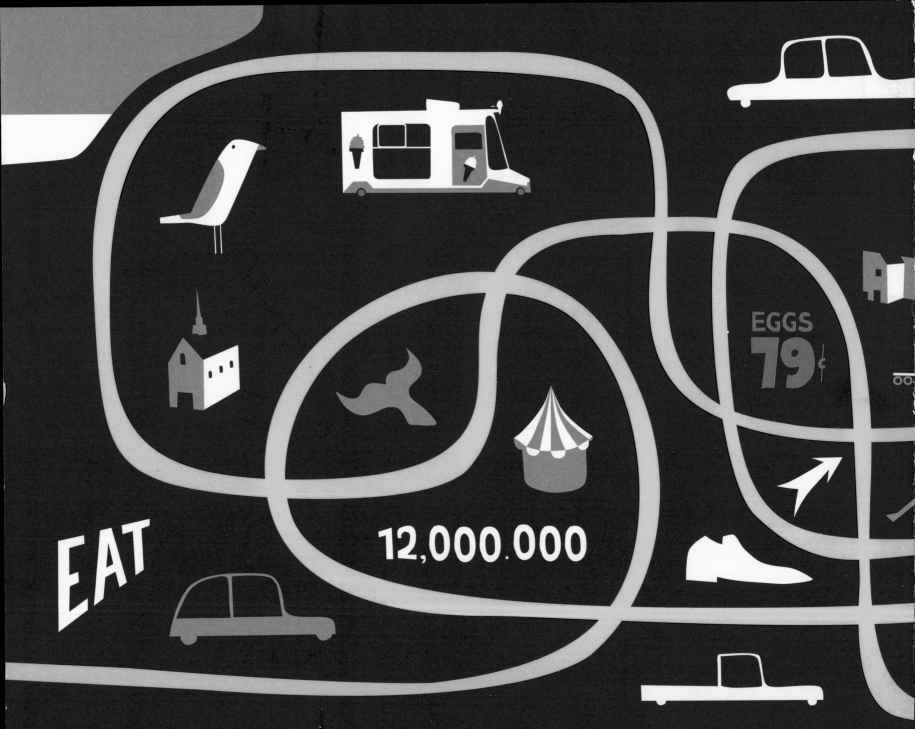